How To be FAMous

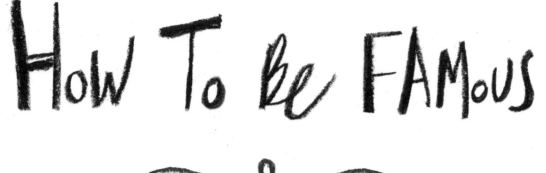

By Michal Shalev

GECKO PRESS

WE HAVE BEEN FAMOUS FOR GENERATIONS.

MY GREAT GREAT GREAT
GREAT GREAT GREAT
GREAT GREAT GREAT GREAT
GREAT GREAT GREAT GREAT
GREAT GREAT GREAT GREAT GREAT GREAT
GREAT GREAT GREAT GREAT GREAT GREAT
GREAT GRANDFATHER
WAS FAMOUS

MY  GREAT GREAT GREAT GREAT GREAT GREAT GREAT GREAT GREAT GREAT GREAT GREAT GREAT GREAT GREAT GREAT

GRANDFATHER WAS FAMOUS

...AND I AM FAMOUS.

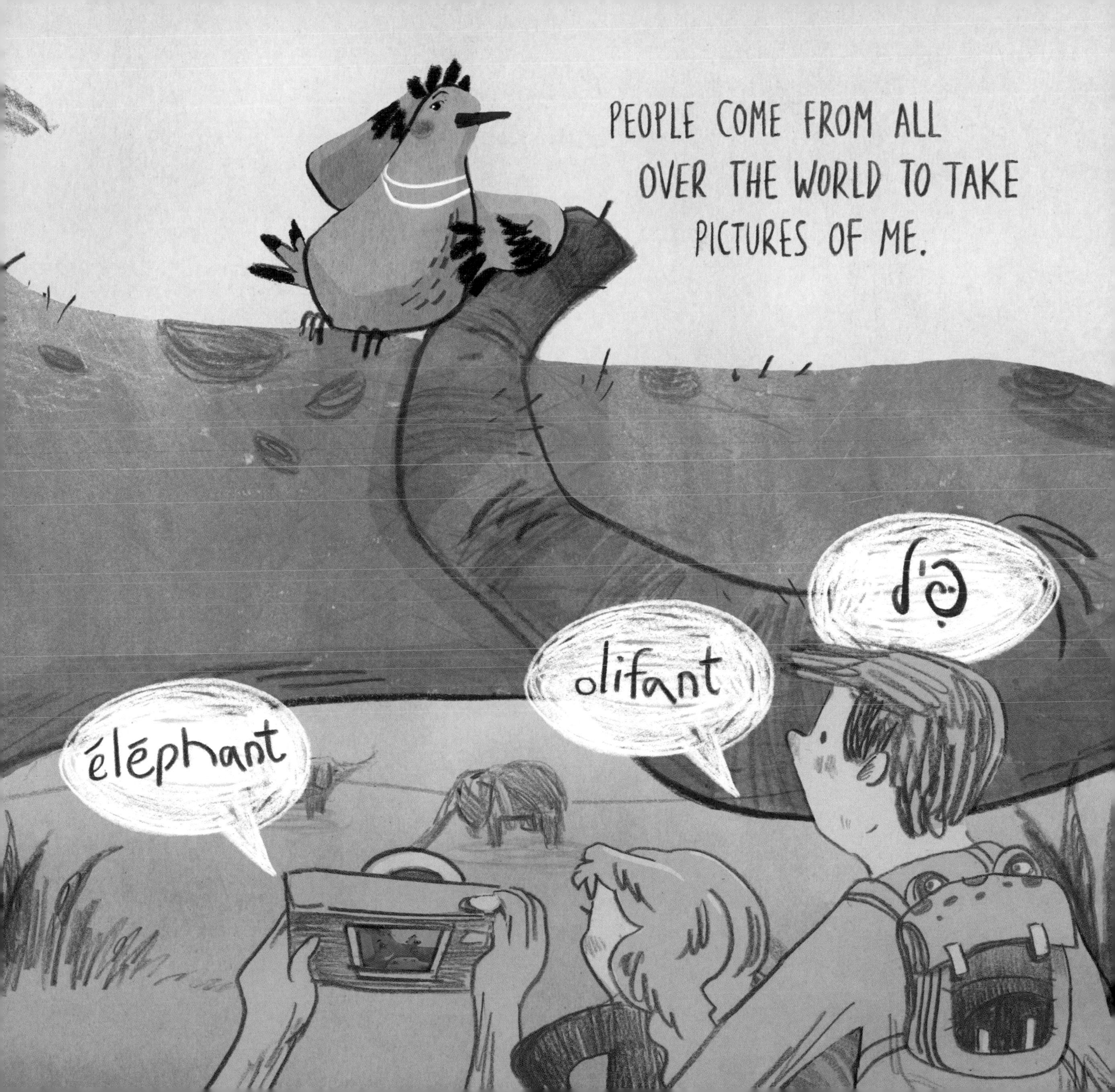

PEOPLE COME FROM ALL OVER THE WORLD TO TAKE PICTURES OF ME.

THEY THINK MY CATWALK IS QUITE SPECTACULAR.

EVERY DAY, I LIKE TO VISIT
THE BEAUTY SALON TO HELP OUT.

AT LUNCHTIME, ALL
THE OTHER ANIMALS
EAT LEFTOVERS...

...BUT I GET TO SIT AT THE TABLE.

EVEN WHEN I AM RESTING,
PEOPLE CONTINUE TO ADMIRE ME.

WHEN PEOPLE SEE ME,
THEY WAVE AND BOW.

IT'S CERTAINLY NOT EASY BEING A TOP MODEL.

I HAVE TO KEEP GOING
WHATEVER THE WEATHER.

AND WHEN THINGS GO WRONG...

...I MUST RISE TO THE OCCASION.

ALL THE OTHER PIGEONS WANT TO BE FAMOUS LIKE ME.

BUT SADLY THEY DON'T HAVE WHAT IT TAKES.

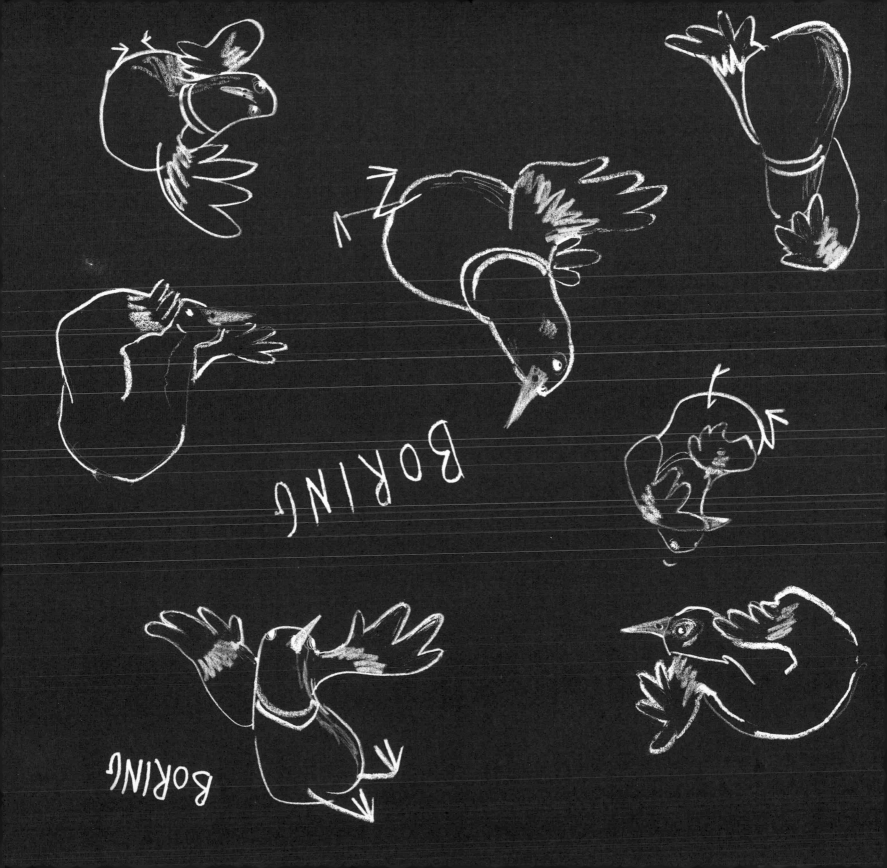

Michal Shalev has studied illustration, animation and graphic design
in Israel and the UK, and has an MA in children's book illustration
from the Cambridge School of Art. She lives in Israel.

This edition first published in 2016 by Gecko Press
PO Box 9335, Marion Square, Wellington 6141, New Zealand
info@geckopress.com

First American edition published in 2016 by Gecko Press USA,
an imprint of Gecko Press Ltd

© Michel Shalev 2016

Distributed in New Zealand by Upstart Distribution, www.upstartpress.co.nz
Distributed in Australia by Scholastic Australia, www.scholastic.com.au
Distributed in the United Kingdom by Bounce Sales & Marketing,
www.bouncemarketing.co.uk
Distributed in the United States and Canada by Lerner Publishing Group,
www.lernerbooks.com

Designed by Vida & Luke Kelly, New Zealand
Printed in China by Everbest Printing Co Ltd,
an accredited ISO 14001 & FSC certified printer

ISBN hardback: 978-1-776570-29-4
ISBN paperback: 978-1-776570-30-0
Ebook available

For more curiously good books, visit www.geckopress.com